Henry Holt and Company, Inc.
Publishers since 1866
115 West 18th Street
New York, New York 10011

Henry Holt is a registered trademark
of Henry Holt and Company, Inc.

Library of Congress Cataloging-in-Publication Data
Klinting, Lars.
Bruno the baker / Lars Klinting.
Summary: Bruno the beaver and his little helper, Felix, carefully follow instructions as they
bake a birthday cake and then get ready to eat it. The recipe is included.
[1. Baking—Fiction. 2. Birthday cakes—Fiction. 3. Cake—Fiction. 4. Beavers—Fiction.]   I. Title.
PZ7.K682Bp 1997 [E]—dc21   97-5120
ISBN 0-8050-5506-1
First American Edition—1997
Printed in China
1 3 5 7 9 10 8 6 4 2
The artist used watercolor and colored pencil to create the illustrations for this book.

LARS KLINTING

BRUNO
the Baker

HENRY HOLT AND COMPANY

NEW YORK

Who is that knocking on Bruno's window?

It's Felix. He has a present for Bruno.
Today is Bruno's birthday.

Bruno loves Felix's flowers.
He wonders if Felix would like to stay for some birthday cake.

Well, first we have to make it!

Here is Bruno's kitchen.
He has lots of pots and pans.
Bruno's grandma gave them to him.
She was a good cook.
What are Bruno and Felix looking for?

Aha! Felix found it—Grandma's cookbook.

Bruno and Felix check the cupboard to see if they have all the ingredients for the cake recipe. They do. Now it's time to get started.

First Bruno melts the butter in a pan.

Next he takes out
the bread crumbs

a basting brush

and a cake pan.

Bruno brushes the inside of the cake pan with some of the melted butter. Then Felix pours some bread crumbs into the pan and shakes it so that the bread crumbs stick to the butter. Bruno turns on the oven.

Now it's time to take out the

sugar

eggs

and Bruno's favorite old bowl.

Bruno cracks the eggs into the bowl.
Felix is a good helper. He adds the sugar.

After Bruno stirs together the sugar and eggs,
he takes out the electric mixer.

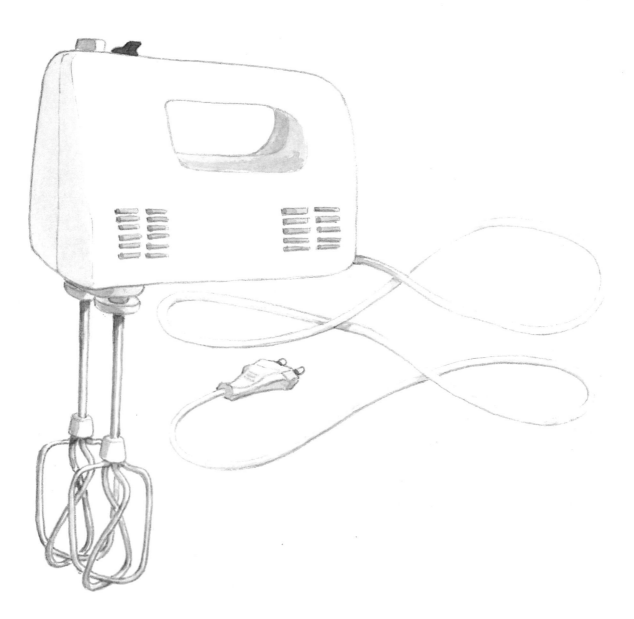

He beats the eggs and sugar until they are fluffy and almost white.
Bruno loves this part. Felix thinks it's too noisy.

Bruno is now ready to mix the

baking soda

confectioners' sugar

and flour.

He blends them together
in a small bowl.

Felix sets aside the mixing spoon

and the milk.

Bruno pours the milk and the rest of the melted butter
into the big bowl with the egg and sugar mixture.
Then Felix adds the contents of the small bowl.
Bruno follows the recipe directions carefully.
The kitchen is getting a little messy but that's okay.

After Bruno and Felix blend the mixture well,
they pour the batter into the cake pan.

The best part of making a cake is licking the bowl.
Felix does this very well.

The cake is ready to bake in the oven.
Bruno wears his oven mitts so he won't get burned.

Felix sets the cake timer.
Then Bruno and Felix sit in front of the oven.
The oven has a glass window and a light
so they can watch the cake bake.
Pretty soon the kitchen is warm and cozy.

After sitting for a while Bruno and Felix decide to clean up.
"Look at the mess we made. We better get to work," says Bruno.

Bruno and Felix wash the dishes while the cake is baking.
The kitchen is soon tidy again.

The cake is done.
Bruno takes it out of the oven and lets it cool for a little while.

After it cools, Felix covers
the cake with a doily...

and places a large plate
on top of the doily.

Abracadabra!

Then Bruno slips one hand under
the cake pan and holds on to the top
as he flips the cake over.

Bruno wiggles the pan a bit and
it comes off. And just look at
that cake! It's perfect!

Now Bruno and Felix take out

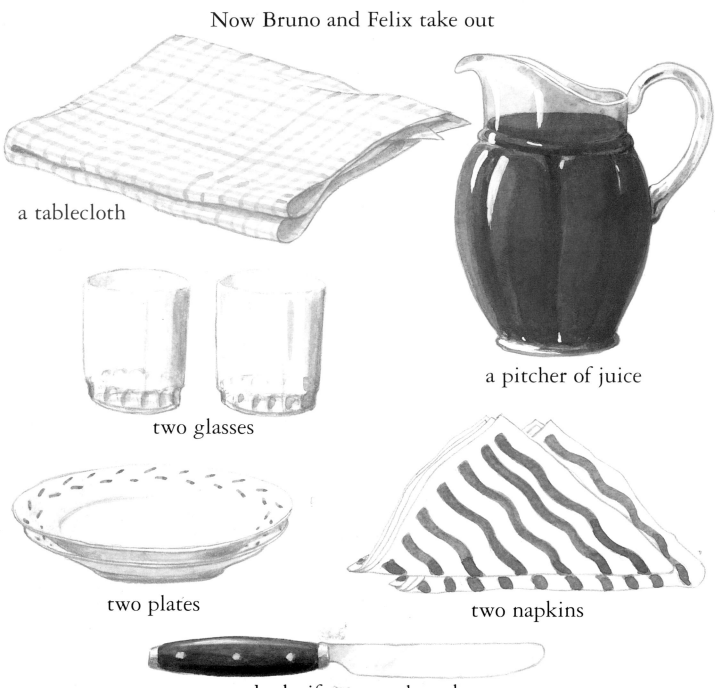

a tablecloth

a pitcher of juice

two glasses

two plates

two napkins

and a knife to cut the cake.

Dingdong!
Just as they finish setting the table
the doorbell rings.
Who can that be?

Happy birthday to you,
Happy birthday to you,
Happy birthday, dear Bruno...

"Hurry, Felix! We'll need more plates and glasses!" says Bruno.

Bruno is happy that his friends
have arrived just in time for cake.
Everyone agrees that the
birthday cake is delicious.
Bruno couldn't have done it
without his little buddy, Felix.

What do you think Bruno
gets as a present?

A beautiful new mixing bowl!

BRUNO'S CAKE

8" x 2" cake pan

5$\frac{1}{3}$ tablespoons butter or margarine
1 tablespoon plain bread crumbs, finely ground
2 large eggs
1 cup granulated sugar
1$\frac{1}{2}$ cups all-purpose flour, sifted
1$\frac{1}{2}$ teaspoons baking soda
1 tablespoon confectioners' sugar
  (or 1 teaspoon vanilla extract)
$\frac{1}{2}$ cup milk

1. Preheat oven to 350° F.
2. Melt the butter in a pan over a low flame.
3. Brush the cake pan with some of the melted butter.
4. Pour the bread crumbs in the cake pan and shake it carefully
   so that the crumbs stick to the sides of the pan.
5. Beat the eggs and sugar together in a large bowl, preferably with an electric mixer,
   until the mixture is fluffy.
6. Combine the flour, baking soda, and confectioners' sugar (or vanilla extract)
   in a small bowl. Stir well (make sure there are no lumps!).
7. Blend milk, remaining butter, and combined flour, baking soda, and confectioners' sugar
   with the egg and sugar mixture in the large bowl, and mix until smooth and creamy.
8. Pour the batter into the cake pan and bake for about 35 minutes. After 35 minutes,
   stick a toothpick in the center of the cake. If it comes out clean, the cake is done.
9. Let the cake sit for 1 hour.

To serve the cake like Bruno: Place a paper doily on top of cake and then place a large plate facedown over the doily. Slip one hand under the cake pan and hold on to the top as you flip the cake over. Lightly wiggle free the pan. Sprinkle the top of the cake with confectioners' sugar.

Yield: 8 pieces of cake